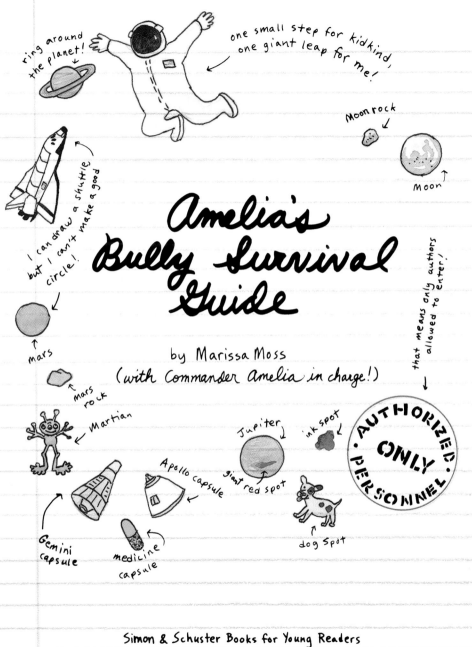

ring around the planet!

one small step for kidkind, one giant leap for me!

Moon rock

Moon

I can draw a shuttle, but I can't make a good circle!

that means only authors allowed to enter!

Amelia's Bully Survival Guide

by Marissa Moss
(with Commander Amelia in charge!)

mars

Mars rock

Martian

Jupiter

ink spot

giant red spot

AUTHORIZED ONLY PERSONNEL

Apollo capsule

Gemini capsule

medicine capsule

dog Spot

Simon & Schuster Books for Young Readers

New York   London   Toronto   Sydney

SIMON & SCHUSTER BOOKS FOR YOUNG READERS
An imprint of
Simon & Schuster Children's Publishing Division
1230 Avenue of the Americas
New York, New York 10020

Copyright © 1998 by Marissa Moss

First SIMON & SCHUSTER BOOKS FOR YOUNG READERS
edition, 2006

Permission to reproduce features of Space Camp®
granted by U.S. Space Camp®.

An Amelia™ Book
Amelia™ and the black-and-white notebook pattern
are trademarks of Marissa Moss.

SIMON & SCHUSTER BOOKS FOR YOUNG READERS
is a trademark of Simon & Schuster, Inc.

Book design by Amelia
(with help from Lucy Ruth Cummins)
Manufactured in Mexico
2 4 6 8 10 9 7 5 3

CIP data for this book is available
from the Library of Congress.

ISBN-13: 978-1-4169-0907-1   ISBN-10: 1-4169-0907-9

← I love getting school supplies! →

↑ new pencils - sharp, sharp, sharp - with that great new pencil smell

fresh, clean, pink erasers (I wish they could stay this way, but I know they'll get all smudgy.)

Tomorrow is my first day as a fifth grader. (I <u>love</u> that sentence — I'm a 5th GRADER!)

Leah has already planned what she's wearing and what's going to be in her lunch. I'm just planning on being excited — and a little nervous. I wonder what my new teacher will be like. Will I like the other kids? Will they like me? Leah's not in my class, but I can still see her at lunch and recess.

new school clothes ↓

new shoes with clean white soles and laces →

great new binder with lots of pockets and dividers because now I'm in 5th grade and I'll need those things →

Leah is <u>so</u> organized, she even knows which barrettes she'll wear (but then, she <u>folds</u> her underwear before putting it away)

my dresser drawer →

Leah's dresser drawer ←

Well, now I know what my teacher is like, and I wish I didn't. Leah gets the <u>good</u> 5th grade teacher, Mr. Reyes — he brought in cookies for the whole class on the first day. I get the witch, Ms. Busby. The first thing she did was read all these rules to us.

new jeans that I need to wash a zillion times until they're old and comfy →

Ms. Busby →

eyebrows that mean business →

mouth pinched tight →

loooong list of rules →

h
ove
If
comp
after
That
We are
means
with co
no teas
no nam
no sho
Ever
by

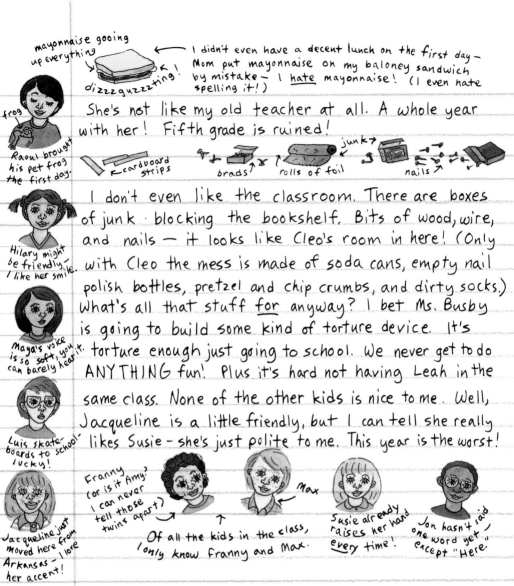

mayonnaise gooing up everything

← I didn't even have a decent lunch on the first day — Mom put mayonnaise on my baloney sandwich by mistake — I <u>hate</u> mayonnaise! (I even hate spelling it!)

dizzzguzzzting!

frog

Raoul brought his pet frog the first day.

She's not like my old teacher at all. A whole year with her! Fifth grade is ruined!

← cardboard strips

brads ↗ ↘

rolls of foil

junk →

nails ↗

I don't even like the classroom. There are boxes of junk · blocking the bookshelf. Bits of wood, wire, and nails — it looks like Cleo's room in here! (Only with Cleo the mess is made of soda cans, empty nail polish bottles, pretzel and chip crumbs, and dirty socks.) What's all that stuff <u>for</u> anyway? I bet Ms. Busby is going to build some kind of torture device. It's torture enough just going to school. We never get to do ANYTHING fun! Plus it's hard not having Leah in the same class. None of the other kids is nice to me. Well, Jacqueline is a little friendly, but I can tell she really likes Susie — she's just polite to me. This year is the worst!

Hilary might be friendly. I like her smile.

Maya's voice is so soft, you can barely hear it.

Luis skateboards to school! lucky!

Jacqueline just moved here from Arkansas — I love her accent!

Franny (or is it Amy? I can never tell those twins apart) ↗

Of all the kids in the class, I only know Franny and Max.

← Max

Susie already raises her hand every time!

Jon hasn't said one word yet except "Here."

Ms. Busby says she's sorry to block the book-case, but she's collecting things for our first science project. I finally get to 5th grade and it's like I'm back in kindergarten, hammering nails into wood and calling it sculpture.

Charlie fell asleep when the rules were read.

Gabe always has his nose in a book.

Carly seems the shyest.

Lucy and Matilda must be best friends — they whisper together CONSTANTLY!

ooooh! what beautiful art!
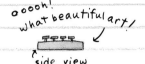
side view

a smiley face — how creative!
top view

Seth keeps sneaking snacks — he smells like popcorn.

All that junk turned out to be not so junky.
We put it all together and made a telegraph.
It was sooo0 cool! I wrote to Nadia and drew
her a picture so she can make her own. I wish
we could tap out messages to each other, but I don't
have a long enough wire.

Brandon jiggles his foot all the time — it's driving me crazy!

I love making inventions.
tap this down and then the brad taps the nail, making a clicking sound
cardboard taped down
foil
wood   foil   battery
wires
brad
cardboard nailed down
wood
nail wrapped with wire
this becomes an electromagnet — wow!

It would have been a perfect day, but at recess, Leah
didn't play with me. She was too busy jumping rope with
Gwen, some girl in her class. I looked for someone I could
jump rope with, but everyone already has a friend
(except Hilary — she was swinging on the bars and I
didn't want to do that).

I guess this notebook is kind of like having a
friend — it listens to what I have to say. But
it doesn't talk back to me (at least we can't
fight that way).

eyebrows that are happy →

← head full of good ideas

friendly smiling mouth →

At least now I like Ms. Busby — she's still strict, but she has good ideas for projects. She says we'll make rockets next! And she _can_ be funny — she's just serious about learning. That's ok — when she does smile, it's great!

Leah won't walk to school with me anymore! She walks with Gwen instead. Just when I start to like school, something rotten happens.

only my shadow sticks by me ↓

Would I look better with hair like this? ↓

or this? ↓

or this? ↓

I really need a friend now, a close-by friend, not a far-away friend like Nadia. I can't believe I ever thought Hilary might be friendly — she's mean, _mean_, MEAN! She said I look like a doofus because I don't wear knee socks and I have a stupid haircut. What's wrong with my hair and why does it matter what kind of socks I wear? But once she said it, everyone else started believing it. Lucy and Matilda wouldn't play four-square with me and when I sat down next to Susie at lunch, she changed places. It was awful.

I _knew_ this would be the worst year of my life!

How about a fancy chocolate chip hairdo? ↓

↑ the problem is none of these look like ME!

Hilary said my hair looks like a mop and I should wash the floor with it. Then she tried to trip me. I wanted to cry, but no _way_ would I EVER let her see me cry.

bathroom mirror ↓

I looked in the mirror for so long my face didn't look like me anymore.

sink ↓

my sister, Cleo, says to slug Hilary hard, but she's never right about anything

Cleo has one tough punch

Mom says to pretend I can't hear what Hilary says – but I hear all the mean things she says too well!

Everyone says you should just ignore teasing and it will go away, but it's _not_ going away. I try to pretend I'm a stone when Hilary talks to me, but inside I feel like I'm crumbling. Why doesn't Leah like me anymore, either? Have I changed somehow? Do I have B.O.?

bad socks
D–

good socks
A+

do socks really matter?

now Hilary says my new shoes are dumb – turns out they're the _wrong_ brand!

I called Leah on the phone and asked what's wrong. She said nothing's wrong, she _still_ likes me, but she's so busy with Gwen, she doesn't have time for _2_ friends. Of course, she picks the person in the same class as her (and Gwen wears knee socks!).
Maybe what I need is a good luck charm.

four-leaf clover

I forgot that Mako, my pen pal, sent me this good luck cat from Japan – so far it hasn't done me much good

Tarot card

Cleo read my fortune with her Tarot cards – she said I will make a new friend. Who? WHO?! When? WHEN?!

why is a cat in a bottle lucky?

rabbit's foot – very _un_lucky for the rabbit!

don't let your luck run out

horseshoe

We started the next science project today –

ROCKETS!

Real ones, not just models We're going to have a big launch day when we're done and see whose flies the best. We have to work with a partner and I held my breath, hoping, hoping, hoping Hilary would NOT be my partner. She's not! She's Seth's partner – what a relief!

Carly is my partner. She likes science as much as I do, and I saw she has a notebook in her desk – it looks like mine!

Carly's notebook ↘

she put stickers all over the cover →

the splotches are green, not black ↘

Today Hilary said my lunch looked gross. Now she's insulting my food. She's always looking for something mean to say.

innocent apple no bruises or worms

bread not moldy ←
no mayonnaise ←

what? you mean I have the wrong kind of chips? ↖

Carly said not to pay attention to Hilary – she's just like that. Carly was in her class last year and Susie was the one Hilary teased then. I'm just the lucky kid this year.

Hilary has a nose with unusually large **noseholes** →

"Excuse me, but are you related to a hippopotamus? Your nose has certain similarities."
I always think of things to say too late.

When Hilary kicked the back of my chair, Carly passed me this note:

Just pretend Hilary is a giant cockroach. Then you won't care what she says or does.

It's funny to imagine Hilary as a cockroach, ↗ but it doesn't make the teasing any easier to take.

At recess, Carly and Maya taught me how to jump Double Dutch. I love it! And it's one game where you need <u>3</u> people instead of just 2.

Carly ↙

me →

my shadow has company now ↓

maya ↘

I wore my crown to the alligator town, I sat on a fence and the fence broke down, the alligator bit me by the seat of the pants, and made me do the hootchie-cootchie dance.

Down by the ocean, down by the sea, Johnny broke a bottle and blamed it on me. I told Ma, Ma told Pa, How many lickings did Johnny get?

So I didn't care when Hilary said I jumped like an elephant (well, not much) because Carly invited me over to her house after school! (And she didn't invite Hilary, so there!)

geode

carnelian

green
aventurine

ulexite

fool's gold

obsidian

Carly has a cool rock collection →

I love the names of rocks and minerals — like "ulexite."
It sounds like a leotard or a small suitcase.

Carly has two big brothers and they're really nice to
her. (I'd trade Cleo for either one of them in a second!)
They brought us soda and chips in her room.
(If I invited Carly to my house, Cleo
would steal snacks from us, not offer
them to us.)

If I throw in a bowl of
chips, would Carly trade
a brother for Cleo?

I like Carly a lot, but I don't want to like her
too much, because what if she starts liking someone
else better, like Leah did?

Carly made me a friendship bracelet like this. I told her
about Leah and she says she's not like that.
↓

I thought the worst was over with Hilary, but it's
not. Today she passed me a note that was so mean
I don't want to write down what it said. Why does
she work so hard to make me cry? What did I do to her?

I memorized every
inch of this desk
↓

blink,
blink

me, staring at my
desk as hard as I
could, so tears would
not come out of my eyes

When some people cry, their mouths look like rubber bands.

Some people's chins wrinkle up.

HONK!
Some people sound like they're blowing their noses.

Mom asked why I'm always cranky now, what's going on. I told her about Hilary's note (but I didn't tell her what it said). She hugged me and pulled me onto her lap even though I'm too big for that anymore. She said kids can be mean. I already knew that. Then she told me a story about grandma Sara I'd never heard before. I want to write it down before I forget it.

Grandma's Story

I never met my grandma, not that I remember, at least. She died when I was little. →

← But I've seen pictures of her. She looked like this.

When Grandma was a kid, it was the Depression (which was a time when nobody in the country had much money because the banks all failed — they couldn't give people their savings back. That can't happen anymore, but it could then and it was <u>terrible</u>.) She was the oldest of 4 girls and it was really hard for her parents to scrape together money to feed the family.

Her father (my great-grandfather) was an engineer — not the train kind, the building kind. He made bridges before the Depression, but he people would stand on the street selling pencils or apples or anything they could think of

lost his job (since nobody had money to pay for building anymore), and the only work he could get was being a janitor in a big office building.

from this ↗   to this ↗

He wasn't paid very much, but at least things were very cheap then. Chicken was 29¢ a pound and bread was 10¢ a loaf.

One day Grandma was sent to the store to buy some bread for bread soup because that was all they could afford for dinner that night. Her mother was sick in bed that day, so Grandma had to go.

She held that dime tight, tight, tight, but on the way a mean boy saw her. He knew she had a coin in her fist.

tough mean boy

worried Grandma Sara

hitting fists, not holding fists

tight fist with dime in it

walking fast without running

He followed her and started to call her names,
then he blocked her way and wouldn't let her go any further.

Grandma was scared and ready to cry. She
wanted to throw the money at the boy and run
away. But then she thought of how mad her
mom would be and how sad her sisters would
be with no dinner. The more she thought,
the madder she got, until she was so mad
at this boy — HOW DARE HE DO THIS! —
that she just BLEW UP!

"Who do you think you are to talk to me like that! You let me pass by NOW!!!"

She yelled so loud, people on the street turned to stare and that mean boy got so scared, <u>he</u> was the one to run away.

She felt like when Alice in Wonderland ate the eat-me cake and grew GIGANTIC.

Now he doesn't feel so big and tough. →

Mama!

← super soup
(but what is bread soup?
soggy bread in broth?)

And Grandma said it was the best dinner she'd had in a long time, even if it was only soup.

The End

Mom said Grandma was a lot like me – she even kept a notebook (but she called it a diary). I asked Mom if I could read it, but she's not sure where it is. It's definitely not in our house somewhere, but she thinks Uncle Frank has it. I'm going to write him and ask. It's cool to think that Grandma wrote and drew things just like me. I wonder if she stuck things in her journal like I do. Did she write stories, too?

old photo of Grandma when she was 8 years old →

this is my story, not Grandma's

The Very Nasty Girl
and Her Awful Fate

Once there was this mean girl who no one liked. She got no presents on her birthday because even her parents hated her. (And she had no brothers or sisters because she was so horrible her parents didn't want to risk having another kid like her.)

One day she got a package in the mail. She was so surprised, she opened it right away. It was a box of chocolates, the fancy kind. She stuffed her face with them. Unfortunately for her they were
∴POISON!∴

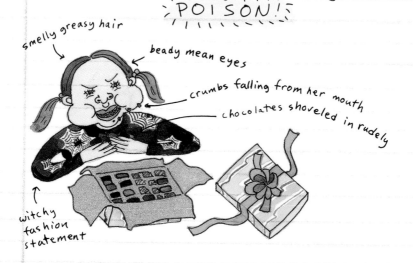

smelly greasy hair

beady mean eyes

crumbs falling from her mouth

chocolates shoveled in rudely

witchy fashion statement

She keeled over and died, and no one bothered to come to her funeral.

Even the grass can't stand to be near her - it turned brown and died.

The other graves stayed far away.

Here lies Nasty Nelly

Definitely The End

Stories always make me feel better. Even if they don't come true.

Good news! Hilary was absent today. (I hope she has the stomach flu _forever_.) Then I came home to even better news — a postcard from Nadia!

Dear Amelia,
 Has Hilary turned into a frog yet? Or a cockroach?
 Guess what? I'm going to Space Camp for winter vacation. Ask your mom if you can come, too. It will be great!
 yours till the banana splits, Nadia

BLAST OFF!

A
M
E
L
I
A

PESTUS 2.7¢
DISGUSTUS
PORTRAIT OF HILARY

564 North
Homerest,
Oopa,
Oregon
97881

Space Camp! I'd LOVE to go to Space Camp. How can I get Mom to say yes?

I tried out my angel act on Mom all weekend. I was SUPER nice to her. I did the laundry. I washed the dishes. I dusted. Cleo was astonished. So was Mom.

angel of housecleaning

sparkling clean dishes

floor clean enough to eat off of

neatly folded clothes— even folded the underwear! (even Cleo's !!)

suspicious Cleo

What's up? There must be something you want.

Mom drinking tea

me, bringing her cookies and the newspaper

Then, when she was all relaxed, drinking the cup of tea I made for her, I asked her about Space Camp.

AND SHE DIDN'T SAY NO!!

She said, "We'll see." But she smiled when she said it. That means YES in Momspeak, at least it usually does.

Today I didn't even care when Hilary called me lizard face. All I could think about was Space Camp, especially when we launched our rockets. It was waaay cool — and in Space Camp you get to do stuff like that EVERY day.

Carly and I decorated our rocket so it would look really good.

we called it the Saturn 2000 — it was one of the highest. (Hilary's rocket only flew half as far and it broke on re-entry.)

When I got home from school, there was an envelope waiting for me and inside of it was

Good for One (1)
Week at Space Camp
(Happy Birthday~this is
your present) very early

HOORAY!

I called Nadia that night. She is _so_ excited. Me, too! I get to be with Nadia _and_ go to Space Camp!

I can't wait to fly in the simulators!

I want to be head of mission control!

Carly said Congratulations. She wishes she could go, too. Her dad said maybe next year.

I thought Cleo would be jealous, but she says who wants to go to dumb Space Camp anyway? You have to work hard there. She only wants to go to Beach Camp or Camp Make-Up-Your-Face. (She's started to wear gunk on her eyelids so she looks like an alien, but in her case,

Cleo without makeup →

Help! A monster! ←

Either way, the mirror cracks.

Cleo with makeup ↗

Help! An alien! ←

it's an improvement.

external fuel tank

solid rocket booster

solid rocket booster

orbiter (what the actual shuttle is called)

I made a calendar to count down the days until Space Camp and I'm reading a book about astronauts and the space shuttle. I hope I get to be the shuttle commander.

T+2 minutes 5 seconds— solid rocket boosters fall off

T+8 minutes 50 seconds — fuel tank separates

T+39 minutes— shuttle in orbit (that's fast!)

Why is it called "T" and not "L" for Lift off? Maybe I'll find out at camp.

T-0-LIFTOFF!

T-6 seconds— main engines start

T-2 hours 30 minutes— crew enters orbiter

T-43 hours— start of countdown

The calendar reminded me I've got to get something for Mako for Christmas. I haven't seen him since last summer at the Grand Canyon, but he's already written me 6 letters (and sent me the good luck charm). Before Carly, he and Nadia were my only friends. (I don't know whether to call Leah a friend or not anymore.) I want to send him something special, something American that he can't get in Japan.

Mako's school photo—he looks just like I remember →

I know what to get Nadia — a rocket kit like the one Carly and I made. ⟶

Cleo says how do I know Mako celebrates Christmas. OK, maybe he doesn't, but it sure feels like the whole world does! Anyway I can always call it a New Year's present. Only what if Japanese New Year isn't January 1st? Does it really matter? I love getting presents ANY time of year.

This candy was in the box from Mako — it looks like fruit snacks, but it's way too pretty to eat.

Mako says this is where his family hangs Christmas stockings — by the bathtub pipe (since they don't have a chimney).

↓ how cozy!

↑ stockings hung by the pipe with care

boy taking a bath

rubber duckie

Japanese bathtub (I imagine)

Before I could send him anything, Mako sent me a Christmas present (way early, but that's OK by me). It turns out he celebrates Christmas and Japanese holidays, so he gave me a beautiful box made from a special paper called Washi. Mako made it himself.

I love reading Mako's descriptions of his holidays. It makes me want to go to Japan and see myself.

Mako sent a photo of his sister, Yumi, dressed up for a November holiday called Shichigosan — it's like an extra birthday only a lot more work. (It took 2 hours just to put on her makeup and get her hair ready.)

almost fell over backwards!

wow — talk about ↑ high heels!

the bow at the back was so heavy, Yumi

My Christmas present to Hilary would be chocolates — very special chocolates. →

I still don't know what to get him. Everything here is so ordinary. (And I can't make any thing like a Washi box.)

jelly beans are kind of pretty, but are they special enough?

↓

↑
I like how they look, but hate how they taste.

I got another letter from Mako — already! He was so excited he had to write me about a new donut store. He'd never tasted a donut before! I never would have thought a donut could be special, but I guess it all depends on what you're used to.

↑
Donuts are another thing that look better than they taste.

You can win prizes when you buy donuts — Mako sent me one of his. →

Tomorrow, I leave for Space Camp and, just in time, I found the PERFECT thing for Mako — it's a notebook, American style, with a set of colored pencils and a bunch of neat erasers. I got the idea from the donuts. Even the most ordinary stuff is different — and cool — when it's from another country. Maybe Mako will send me a Japanese notebook someday. I'd LOVE that.

donut song:
Oh! I ran around the corner and I ran around the block and I ran right into a donut shop and I picked up a donut and I wiped off the grease and I handed the lady a 5-cent-piece. Well, she looked at the nickel and she looked at me and she said "This nickel's no good to me, there's a hole in the middle and it goes right through," and I said "There's a hole in the donut, too! Thanks for the donut. Bye now!"

Mako's new notebook — I copied the recipe for donuts from Mom's cookbook and put it in here (along with a copy of the donut song (with pictures, of course).
↓

← My bag is all packed and ready.

I'm so excited, I can't sleep. Tomorrow I'll be in a dormitory (only at Space Camp, it's called a Habitat). I've never slept in a room with a bunch of strangers before (although I've shared a room with Cleo and she's _very_ strange). I wonder what the showers will be like. And will the food be good or will it be gross cafeteria food? I hope it's astronaut food — that would be cool!

Do astronauts use forks or do they just squeeze food into their mouths?

Dig in! ↓

← astronaut spaghetti

astronaut ice cream →

does

Every meal comes in little foil pouches so it all looks the same — does it taste the same?

I'm sure I won't miss Cleo, but I'm a little worried about missing Mom — and my room. When we first moved here I hated this room. Now I love it.

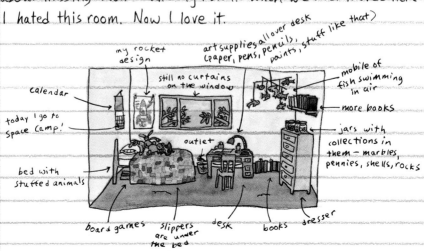

my rocket design

art supplies all over desk (paper, pens, pencils, paints, stuff like that)

still no curtains on the window

mobile of fish swimming in air

calendar

more books

today I go to Space Camp!

jars with collections in them — marbles, pennies, shells, rocks

outlet

bed with stuffed animals

board games

slippers are under the bed

desk

books

dresser

OFFICIAL SPACE CAMP LOG

Nadia was waiting for me when we got there (it was a looooooong drive — we got up so early it was still night out). I got the bunk next to hers and we're both on Triton team.

So far I'm too excited to get homesick. (But Mom cried when she kissed me goodbye — she said she misses me already and she made me promise to call her EVERY night.)

We can hold hands and whisper to each other at night.

Nadia

me

my badge

my team button

AMELIA

Triton is one of Neptune's moons — it has volcanoes and snow.

TRITON

Triton is the only moon that travels in the opposite direction of Neptune's orbit.

space camp pen ↓

We get a pen and a notebook so we can write
important stuff down. ↑

We're so busy training, today is the first chance I've had
to write in here. (At least I haven't had time to get
homesick, either — just a little bit at lunch and dinner
because we <u>don't</u> get astronaut food. We get gross
cafeteria food <u>three</u> times a day.)

Breakfast is ok.
it's hard to ruin
cereal and hot
chocolate. →

First thing we did was get assigned
our positions for flight crew and ground control. Besides
Nadia and me, there's only one other girl on our team, Olena.
(It's funny, but there are way more boys than girls at Space
Camp.) Olena wasn't sure what she wanted to be, but
Nadia definitely wanted to be flight director — that's the
person in charge of mission control on the ground — and
I wanted to be commander, the one in charge of the
flight crew. Brad, Evan, and Corey wanted to be
commander, too, and they said there was no way I'd
get to be commander because I'm a girl and no girl
has ever led a shuttle mission.

Not yet, I said.

mission
specialist?

payload specialist?

Do I want to
be the pilot?

ground control
officer?

Olena making up her mind →

We had to write down our choices and why we wanted that position. Then we had to answer questions about what we've learned so far. Luther, our counselor, would pick the people with the best answers for each job.

Brad, Evan, and Corey were fighting with each other over which of them would get to be commander — they didn't bother with me because they said there was no way I'd be chosen.

MASTIF—Multiple Axis Space Test Inertia Facility

Simulates capsule out of control, tumbling in outer space — it looks like it would make you dizzy, but it doesn't.

MMU — Manned Maneuvering Unit →

simulates frictionless space you would have in actual MMU — the MMU allows short untethered space walks.

It hovers off the ground — you fly!

We have a <u>lot</u> of training to do to get ready for our shuttle mission. I'll be commander of Discovery. It will be tricky because Luther says something is going to go wrong during our mission (only he won't say what), and we'll have to figure out how to correct the problem.

If we can't solve the problem, we either have to abort the mission (that means cancel it and just return to earth) or we'll crash. Or we might solve it the WRONG way, which means we'll also crash.

Microgravity Simulator — this trains astronauts for moonwalks — you can try different steps. I liked the slow motion jog the best, Nadia liked the bunny hop.

Spinning chair ↓

used to test reaction times after being disoriented by spinning — definitely a barf simulator for Cleo

NASA loves LAs — that means Long Acronyms, not a city in California.

SSMT — Space Station Mobility Trainer ↘

This is like a treadmill for zero gravity — your body can even be upside-down! I felt like a hamster on a wheel on it.

Gemini capsule

Mercury capsule

Apollo capsule

It's going to be even harder than I thought, because Brad, Corey, and Evan won't listen to me. They say I'm not really commander and they will <u>never</u> take orders from a girl. (But I bet they listen to their moms.) They're ruining <u>everything</u>.

outside view

it looks like a real shuttle

this is where we do our missions

mission specialist sits here

you come out of the hatch here

hatch – you climb in here

payload specialist sits here

inside view

commander sits here

control panels

pilot sits here

storage lockers and sleep compartments are on the lower deck

we even get to wear cool headsets so we can talk to mission control

shuttle meals look like this – it turns out you eat with a knife, fork, and spoon even in space

unfortunately, it's still gross cafeteria food – weightlessness does not help the taste

the food is in individual plastic compartments you need to cut open

this how you wash your hands in space – no baths or showers (that part might be good)

turns water hot and cold

engine goes in here

rocket separates here in flight and chute comes out

shock cord

nose cone

cricket goes in this clear payload bay

fins →

parachute in body for landing

Today we made rockets like Carly and I did at school, only this time there's a clear hollow tube attached to the nose cone. We're going to put a cricket in there and we were supposed to figure out how to build the rocket so that it will launch and land without hurting the cricket.

I hope Evan's rocket crashes into Brad's, whose rocket will splat into Corey's, and they'll all three explode. (Sorry, crickets!)

cricket astronaut, or cricketnaut →

← If my rocket went all the way to Mars, there'd be cricket life on Mars!

I called Mom — at last. I know I promised to call everyday, but we're so busy and there's always a looong line at the pay phone after dinner. It was great to hear her voice. I even liked talking to Cleo.

You can only talk for 5 minutes, but the line is still loooooooong.

Some kids are really homesick — they don't have a friend like I have Nadia and they say it's too much here. The work is hard, but it's the good kind of hard.

my turn at last!

We had a field trip to NASA in the morning - it was really cool. We got to see a real astronaut training in simulators!

Even the bus ride was great - it was the kind of bus with TV sets in it.

After lunch, we launched our rockets. My cricket landed safely! So did Nadia's. Only two crickets fell out when their rockets broke on landing (the parachutes got stuck so instead of gently floating down, they crashed to the ground). One was Olena's, the other was Brad's. (That shows what a rotten commander he would be.)

My cricket didn't make it to Mars, but it got a nice view of Space Camp from high up.

Tomorrow is our shuttle mission and I'm getting really nervous. I heard that Andromeda team blew up on re-entry because the commander forgot to close the payload doors and Callisto team didn't put down the landing gear so they crashed. There's so much to remember! Evan is the pilot, so he's supposed to help me, but I don't know if I can count on him. Brad is payload specialist and Corey is part of ground control so they don't matter as much. At least I have Nadia as flight director. I know I can depend on her.

I've got to sleep so I'll be alert tomorrow.

I keep seeing the control panels in my head, imagining everything that can go wrong.

DISCOVERY MISSION

So much has happened, I'm not sure where to start. We lifted off ok (and it felt _so_ real!). The boosters and fuel tank separated the way they were supposed to, but Evan kept calling me Salamander Amelia instead of <u>Commander</u> Amelia. I got really steamed and that's bad because being mad is distracting and I <u>had</u> to pay attention.

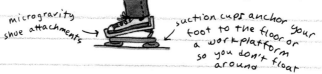

microgravity shoe attachments →

suction cups anchor your foot to the floor or a workplatform so you don't float around

Even with Evan being a jerk, we deployed a satellite and Olena, the mission specialist, ran her experiments. So far our mission was a success— <u>no</u> mistakes. Then just as we were about to start our deorbit maneuver, an alarm went off— <u>both</u> our orbital maneuvering engines had failed!

Evan went into a total panic. "We're gonna die! We'll be lost in space forever!" He wouldn't stop screaming. Olena was frozen in her chair. I could hear Nadia in mission control saying, "Oh no, oh no."

I wanted to scream

STAY CALM

but instead my voice got very low and quiet. It didn't even sound like my voice anymore — it was **SHARP** and **HARD** and **GRAY**. All the other kids looked at me with big eyes and Evan stopped screaming.

It was amazing — I felt big and powerful because of that VOICE that you just had to listen to.

I said slowly and calmly, "We're NOT going to panic. We can still land safely." But I wasn't sure how.

Nadia said we could stay in orbit for 15 more minutes, but we had to decide what to do by then. In real life, we could orbit for days. In the simulator, we had to finish by lunch so the next team could go in. Only 15 minutes! That's less time than a math test.

I never thought of voices before, but they really matter a lot. → 🧀🐭 ← If you have a squeaky voice, people think you're as timid as a mouse.

If you have a cartoony voice, no one takes you seriously.

If you have a scratchy voice, people think you're a witch.

If you have a croaky voice, people think you're a frog (and they're right!).

I thought and thought and thought. I tried to remember _everything_ we'd learned. (What kept popping into my head was how to go to the bathroom in space — _that_ was no help.)

    Evan, Brad, and Olena kept looking at me, not saying anything, just waiting. Then I had an idea. Maybe if we fired the smaller maneuvering rockets, we could use them instead of the orbital engines to break the orbit and push us back through earth's atmosphere. We'd just have to fire the rockets longer since they were smaller, but how long would be long enough?

Nadia agreed this was our best bet, but I could hear how worried she was. →

    No one knew how long we would need to burn the rockets. I would have to guess. Since a regular burn lasts from 2 to 3 minutes, I decided we would try 9 minutes.

    We belted ourselves in and Evan fired the rockets. Those were 9 loooooooong minutes. I felt like I was holding my breath the whole time.

IT WORKED!

We landed just fine (I remembered the landing gear, of course), and when we came out of the shuttle, everyone at mission control stood up and applauded.

I felt like a hero.

Nadia hugged me. She said she was so proud of me. And for the rest of Space Camp, Brad, Evan, and Corey totally stopped teasing me. Even better, when it was time for graduation, Triton team won the award for most successful mission!

the last day I got to wear my wings

pin for most → successful mission

Nadia bought me this patch at the gift shop as a goodbye present she said I definitely earned it.

It was hard saying goodbye to Nadia, especially since it meant going back to school — and seeing Hilary again. But it feels great to be home (I even gave Cleo a hello kiss —

she was astonished!)

Mom promised we'd have a celebration dinner of pizza (what I missed the most at Space Camp), but first I wanted to be alone in my room for a while.

I had to say hello to all my old stuff.

familiar lamp

old favorite bear

colored pencils I've made a million drawings with

I'm saving stamps so I can write lots of letters to Nadia (I'm so glad she's still my friend) — and I need to write Mako about Space Camp.

Going back to school was definitely not easy. I didn't want to go from being a hero to being a jerk (as Hilary calls me).

me walking to school as slowly as possible, all alone again

Space Camp shirt

counting the cracks in the sidewalk to see which comes first — 100 cracks or the gate to school

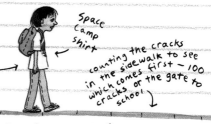

I looked for Carly, but the first thing I saw was Hilary's nasty face, like she was waiting for me.

Well, if it isn't the doofus!

Luckily, the bell rang before she could say anything else.

Unluckily, Ms. Busby gave us a surprise test first thing!

loooong test

OK, class, let's see how much math you remember. You have 30 minutes.

I didn't remember much math. First Hilary, then a math test — it was a rotten day. And it got even worse. At recess, I could see Hilary waiting for me, so I tried to ignore her. But she wouldn't let me.

Miss Mary Mack, Mack, Mack

me keeping an eye out for Hilary

Carly

All dressed in black, black, black

Hilary's squinty mean eyes →

She grabbed my elbow and said, "I saw you cheating on that test, worm breath — CHEATER!"

Hilary has said <u>lots</u> of mean things to me, but this was <u>the worst</u>. Maybe that's why for once I didn't feel all sad and crumbly inside. I was MAD — I mean, really, REALLY, REALLY

FURIOUS!

I looked right at her and said in my new SHARP and HARD and GRAY voice,

"You are a lying fink." And once I started, I couldn't stop. It was like all this stuff came bubbling up inside of me and just <u>had</u> to come out.

"You are nasty, NAS<u>TY</u>, NAS<u>TY</u>. I DID NOT cheat. I don't <u>need</u> to cheat. And there's <u>nothing</u> wrong with my hair or my shoes or my clothes. The only thing wrong with me is that I ever let <u>you</u> bug me. But you're never going to bug me again — you're going to

BUG OFF!

Then I turned and walked away.
I wanted to look back and see if she
was following me, but I was too afraid
to, so I just kept going till I found a
tree to hide behind and then I sat down.
I was exhausted and empty like I'd run
a million miles. Then I felt lighter
and lighter, like I could fly (without the
shuttle even!).

Hilary bug

Carly told me that when I walked away,
Hilary started to bawl. She sounded just
like a cow!

Hilary all alone
on the playground

Carly said she
had a rubber band
mouth and a crinkly chin.

All the bad stuff I
held in bubbled up, out, and awaaay!

I almost felt sorry for her. Almost.

Dear Nadia,
  School feels
~~wierd weird wierd~~ aaagh! ↙
wierd after Space
Camp. But in one
BIG way, it's a lot
better than before
vacation.
  Hilary <u>doesn't tease
me anymore</u> - ~~it feels~~ GREAT!

Nadia Kurz
61 South St.
Barton, CA
91010

yours till
saturn rings,
amelia ♡

↑ I wrote my good news to Nadia

    More good things that happened today: Carly
invited me to sleep over this Saturday, Leah
shared her fruit snacks with me at lunch, and
Hilary hasn't even <u>looked</u> at me since I told
her off. (Why didn't I do that <u>months</u> ago?!)
    And the best news is Uncle Frank found
my grandma's diary, and he's sending it to
me so I can read it. I wonder if the bread
soup story is in it.

I guess I didn't need a
new hairdo — is this what
a commander looks
like — me?
↘